About the Author

C. Foster is a father who cherishes his time reading books to his little girl. With a gift for bringing his imagination to life, he wrote the children's book series, Camille The French Toad. The unique rhythm of his books combined with page into page action totally captivated children, and he is excited to introduce Camille to the world!

Camille The French Toad

C. Foster

Illustrated by Mel Albino

Camille The French Toad

www.camillethefrenchtoad.com

www.olympiapublishers.com
OLYMPIA PAPERBACK EDITION

A CIP catalogue record for this title is
available from the British Library.

ISBN: 978-1-78830-572-3

This is a work of fiction.
Names, characters, places and incidents originate from the writer's imagination. Any resemblance to actual
persons, living or dead, is purely coincidental.

First Published in 2020

Olympia Publishers
Tallis House
2 Tallis Street
London
EC4Y 0AB

Printed in Great Britain

Dedication

For my daughter Emily, grow up slowly……Please!

Here I go more fast than slow all the way
down the long road.

Up and down with a smile no frown,
I am Camille the French Toad.

I jumped on a lily pad and now I am really sad
this pad had a mouth.

I'm in the belly of a fish, this is not what I wish
and I'm quickly heading south!

I sang a high note and sprung from his throat
all the way up in the air.

Oh no a bee I've been stung on my knee
this just isn't fair!

I yelled to the otter and he replied, "What's the matter?
"Please pull this stinger out of me."

The otter yanked hard and fell back a yard
all the way to the apple tree.

We sat for a bite and now the days looking bright.
"Mr. Otter I'm glad we had met."

I hopped in the grass but I had better think fast
because here comes a boy with a net.

Sacrableu I'm too slow, little boy let me go
I don't want to be toad leg stew.

"Dinner for pappy he will be ever so happy,
he's going to fricassee and eat you."

Back at the house I saw Franswa the Mouse.
"Franswa, please chew the bottom of the net."

He chewed out a hole and I slid down the pole,
this is sure a day I'd like to forget.

I hopped on the floor and was heading for the door
when Franswa let out a big yell.

"Camille over here the cat is coming near
I'm running outside towards the well."

The cat stood on the well, slipped on the side and he fell. We can't just leave him down there.

We sent down a hat and pulled up the wet cat and
helped him dry off his hair.

So here we go more fast than slow
all the way down the long road.

With Franswa the Mouse and the Cat from the House
and I am Camille the French Toad.

9 781788 305723